P9-CWD-865

Where Is Little Reynard?

by Joyce Carol Oates

illustrated by Mark Graham

HarperCollinsPublishers

Where Is Little Reynard?   Text copyright © 2003 by Ontario Review, Inc.   Illustrations copyright © 2003 by Mark Graham

Manufactured in China. All rights reserved.   www.harperchildrens.com

Library of Congress Cataloging-in-Publication Data

Oates, Joyce Carol, date.   Where is Little Reynard? / by Joyce Carol Oates ; illustrated by Mark Graham.   p.   cm.

Summary: When Little Reynard, the only orange kitten in his litter, meets some foxes, he feels more at home with them than with his own family.

ISBN 0-06-029559-7 — ISBN 0-06-029583-X (lib. bdg.)   [1. Cats—Fiction. 2. Foxes—Fiction. 3. Family—Fiction. 4. Identity—Fiction.]

I. Graham, Mark, date, ill. II. Title.   PZ7.O1056 Li 2003   2001039501   [E]—dc21   CIP   AC

Design by Stephanie Bart-Horvath   1 2 3 4 5 6 7 8 9 10   ❖   First Edition

Again, for Lily, Jeanne, and Dan
—J.C.O.

For Daisy and Lily
—M.G.

Momma Cat had seven kittens:

1 BOOTS

2 FLUFFY

3 SWEETPEA

4 MIDNIGHT

5 SNOWBALL

6 TWINKLE

and **7** LITTLE REYNARD

The cat family lived with the Smiths

in a big house in the woods.

Mr. and Mrs. Smith had one little girl:

LILY.

Lily loved all the kittens, but she loved
Little Reynard most of all. He was the only
orange kitten in the litter, and he was so
small, he could ride on Lily's shoulder and
even hide in Mrs. Smith's sewing box.

But his sisters laughed at his unusual color. And his brothers teased him because he was so small. This made him shy. Sometimes he meowed so softly that no one heard him—

except LILY.

At dinnertime Boots and Fluffy and Sweetpea and Midnight and Snowball and Twinkle were so hungry, they didn't notice that Little Reynard was too timid to reach the dinner bowl.

But Lily saw, and she gave Little Reynard

his own special bowl.

At playtime Little Reynard sat on Lily's shoulder and watched the other kittens play their favorite games. He wanted to play with them, but he didn't dare.

One afternoon on a cold winter day, Little Reynard discovered a window open and climbed onto the sill to sniff the air. What a surprise he saw! In the woods close to the house, a mother fox was grooming her cubs,

and they looked like HIM.

One of the cubs peered into the window
at Little Reynard. "Hello! I'm Rusty," he
said. "Are you a little fox like me?"

Little Reynard was so surprised, he said,
"Yes! I am."

The second little fox peered into the
window too. "What's your name?" she
asked. "Mine is Flora."

"I'm Little Reynard," said Little Reynard.

"Little Reynard, come play with us!" the foxes cried.

Little Reynard said, "Yes! I will play with you!" Then, forgetting to be shy, he climbed out the window and ran off into the woods with his new friends.

They went sledding
on their tails!

They went skating on
the frozen pond!

They went flying on
the wind!

Little Reynard had never had such fun.

Meanwhile, Momma Cat and all six
kittens were looking for Little Reynard. Lily was
looking too. The cats looked in the attic, and in
the playroom, and behind the stairs. Lily looked
in her mommy's sewing box, and in her own bed.

"Oh, Little Reynard! Where are you?" she cried.

Hours passed, and still Little Reynard played with the little foxes. His fur grew sleek and handsome from the cold, and his tail fluffed out like a fox's brush. He didn't feel the least bit shy!

The moon rose, and Rusty and Flora and Little Reynard continued playing. Then Little Reynard heard a voice calling through the woods. "Little Reynard, where are you?"

It was Lily!

"I have to go home now," said Little Reynard, and he ran back to the Smiths' house. When he got there, the window was closed! He peered into the kitchen and was surprised to see that his six brothers and sisters were not playing at all, and Momma Cat and Lily had never looked so sad.

"Why, I'm not a little fox. I'm a kitten!" Little Reynard said to himself. Then he leaped onto the front porch and meowed.

Everybody in the house heard! But
it was Lily who ran to open the door.

Everybody was so happy to see him!
Momma Cat ran to her lost kitten and licked
him clean right away, with extra kisses.

Then Boots and Fluffy and Sweetpea and
Midnight and Snowball and Twinkle took
turns kissing him. They had missed him so!

Little Reynard waved good-bye to the
Fox family from the window. They would
always be his friends, he knew.

Always after this, Little Reynard played with the other kittens.

For he was as big as any of them now. AND he was proud of it.

The Smiths gave him a special dinner, and Lily brought him to sleep on her pillow that night. "Where were you, Little Reynard?" she whispered. But Little Reynard just curled near Lily's shoulder and PURRED.